SOME
STUFF

Library of Congress Cataloging-in-Publication Data
Ring, Elizabeth, 1920—
Some stuff / by Elizabeth Ring ; illustrated by
Anne Canevari Green.
p.   cm.
Summary: A new neighbor comes over to play and
a young girl almost overwhelms him when she shows
him all her stuff.
ISBN 1-56294-466-5
[1. Play—Fiction.   2. Stories in rhyme.]
I. Green, Anne Canevari, ill.   II. Title.
PZ8.3.R4725So   1995
[E]—dc20   94-26196   CIP   AC

Published by The Millbrook Press Inc.
2 Old New Milford Road
Brookfield, Connecticut 06804

BY ELIZABETH RING

SOME STUFF

ILLUSTRATED BY
ANNE CANEVARI GREEN

THE MILLBROOK PRESS • BROOKFIELD, CONNECTICUT

It's a jump-around, yell-and-shout,

blue-and-white day.

But not
a friend
on the
block
can come
out to
play.

No
place
to go.

Nothing
to do.

What's your name? . . . Jerome?
My name's Lenore. Are you moving
into that new house next door?

You
want
to
come
in?

I'll
show
you
my
stuff.

Here. Hold my kitty. Her name is Snuff.

And look. See my store?

And here's Dottie—my doll.

And this is her buggy.

You
can
bounce
my
ball!

My rocking horse goes!

My kangaroo.

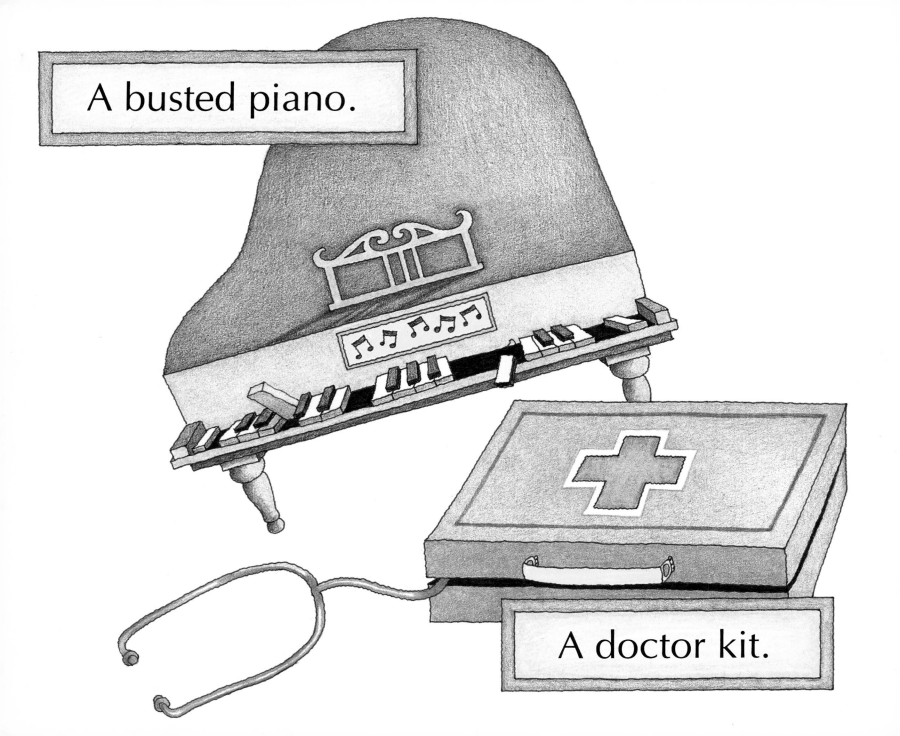

Paper and crayons.

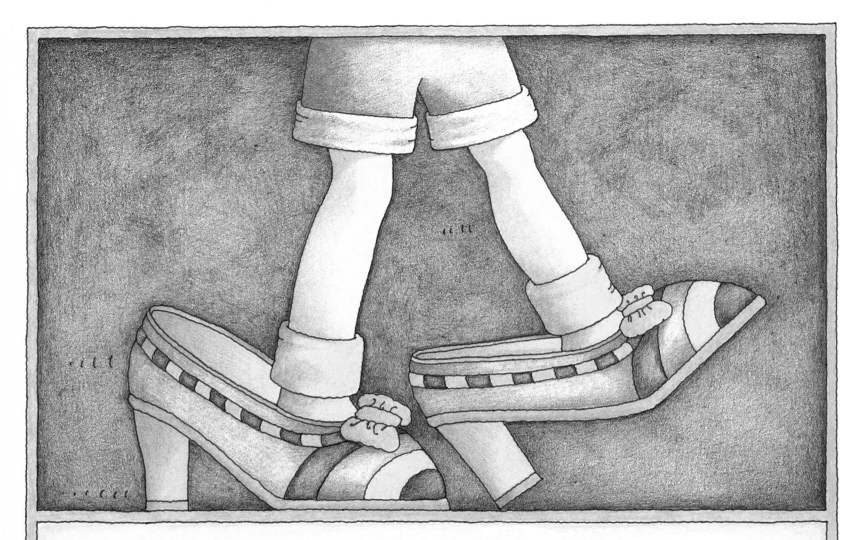

And high heels.
They fit.

My bunny hat from dancing school.

Skates.

And a
tea set.

My
old
wading
pool.

Bird cage.

Puppets.

Paints!

Oh! Jerome
went away!

Now why
did he go?

I wanted
someone to
play with so.

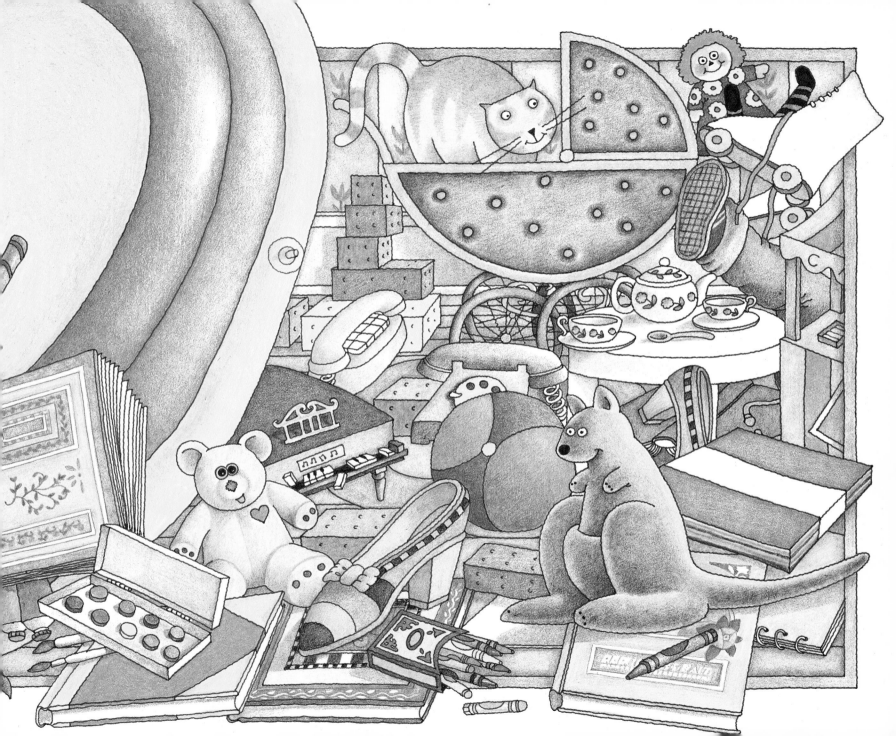

What did you say?

You'd rather go someplace else to play?

Okay. Out in the yard I've got . . . .

Or maybe you'd rather . . . .

I'll tell you what:

Let's just go out and play in the sun.

You tell *me* what *you* think would be fun.

ABOUT THE AUTHOR

Elizabeth Ring has written poetry, stories, plays, and nonfiction books and articles for adults and children. Her previous books for young readers include two picture books, *Night Flier* and *Tiger Lilies and Other Beastly Plants;* two biographies, *Rachel Carson: Caring for the Earth* and *Henry David Thoreau: In Step With Nature;* the Good Dogs! series, a group of eight books on working dogs; and *Two Feet, Four Feet,* a collection of stories.

She is a former editor and a frequent contributor to *Ranger Rick,* the National Wildlife Association's magazine for children, and lives in Woodbury, Connecticut.

ABOUT THE ILLUSTRATOR

Anne Canevari Green has illustrated over fifty books for young readers. Raised in East Norwalk, Connecticut, she took her art training at the College of New Rochelle, and worked for many years as a book designer/illustrator at McGraw-Hill publishers in New York City.

She and her husband, Monte, now live and work in a seaside cottage in Westhampton Beach, Long Island, New York.